Per RFP 03764 Follett School Solutions guarantees
hardcover bindings through SY 2024-2025
877.899.8550 or customerservice@follett.com

Discarded

To
....

HAPPY EASTER

Love
....

W9-AGP-284

THE EASTER BUNNY
is coming to
NEW YORK

Written by Eric James   Illustrated by Mari Lobo

sourcebooks
wonderland

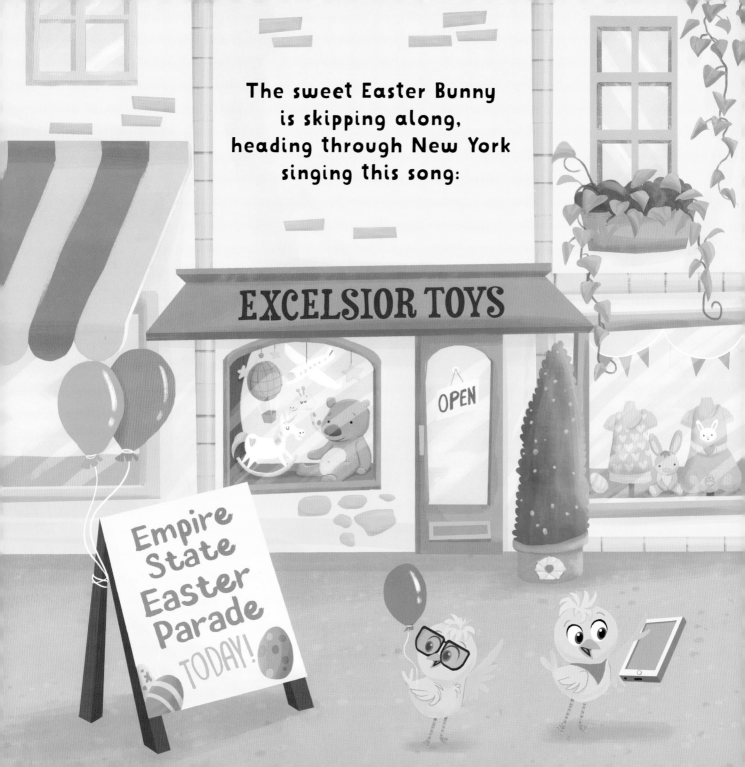

The sweet Easter Bunny
is skipping along,
heading through New York
singing this song:

EXCELSIOR TOYS

OPEN

Empire
State
Easter
Parade
TODAY!

"The eggs are delivered.
My Easter job's done.
And now it is time
that I joined in the fun!"

She jumps down a tunnel
that runs underground,
and pops up again
in each city and town.

Jamestown, Albany,
the Adirondacks, too.
I bet there's a tunnel
that's very near you!

In New York City young children
have smiles on their faces,
and eggs decorated
like people and places!

EASTERN
BLUEBIRD
PARK

But one little boy
drops the egg from his hands.
A loud **CRACKING** sound
can be heard as it lands.

"**Oh dear!**" says the bunny,
and dabs at a tear.
"You need cheering up
so thank goodness I'm here!"

She wiggles her ears,
she hops on the spot,
she waggles her tail,
and he giggles a lot!

In Rochester, there is
an Easter parade.
Most children are clapping
but one looks afraid.

That clapping is noisy.
These legs are so TALL!
It's crowded and loud,
and she's ever so small!

"Gee whiz, what a din!
I know just what to do.
Come here little one
and I'll hold hands with you!"

She wiggles her ears,
and spins her around.
The little girl laughs
as her feet leave the ground!

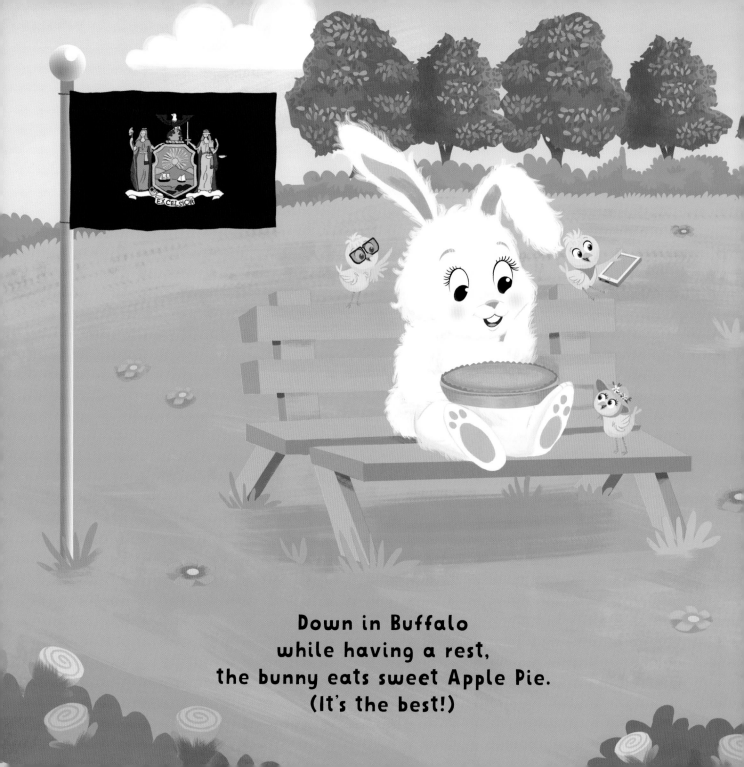

Down in Buffalo
while having a rest,
the bunny eats sweet Apple Pie.
(It's the best!)

Across in the park
there's an egg-rolling race.
A small boy falls down
and he's now lost his place!

She's just a big blur
as she tumbles on past.
The boy runs to help her.
He's going so FAST!

FINISH

She wiggles her ears,
he can't (but he tries!).
They hop up and down
for they've just won first prize!

In Syracuse, a girl's lost
her favorite stuffed bear.
Where could she have left him?
She's looked everywhere!

"When I'm feeling sad
do you know what I do?
I hop up and down!
Do you want to try too?"

She wiggles her ears, the girl thinks it's funny,
and laughs even more when she hops like a bunny!

They both jump around like they haven't a care.
And look what the chicks have just found, over there!

In Cooperstown, the bunny
helps children with SHARING.

In Seneca Falls, she helps a child
to be DARING.

In Poughkeepsie she SINGS,
in Lake Placid she WIGGLES.

Wherever she goes
she brings LAUGHTER and GIGGLES!

This day's been so busy
but also such fun.
The bunny daydreams
in the warm setting sun.

The twilight is coming,
the three chicks are lazing,
and tweeting about
how this day's been #AMAZING!

More chocolate needs making!
New eggs will need wrapping!
It's all so exciting,
the three chicks start flapping!

"New York is great
and we love being here.
We'll make lots more eggs
and we'll be back
next year!"

She wrinkles her nose,
she wiggles her ears,
she blows you a kiss,
and she just...disappears!

Written by Eric James
Illustrated by Mari Lobo
Additional artwork by Gisela Bohórquez
Designed by Nicky Scott

Copyright © Hometown World Ltd. 2019

Sourcebooks and the colophon are registered trademarks of Sourcebooks, Inc. All rights reserved. No part of this book may be reproduced in any form or by any electronic or mechanical means including information storage and retrieval systems—except in the case of brief quotations embodied in critical articles or reviews—without permission in writing from its publisher, Sourcebooks, Inc.

Published by Sourcebooks Wonderland,
an imprint of Sourcebooks Kids
P.O. Box 4410, Naperville, Illinois 60567-4410
(630) 961-3900
sourcebookskids.com

Date of Production: August 2019
Run Number: 5015369
Printed and bound in China (1010)
10 9 8 7 6 5 4 3 2 1